BEWARE!!
DO NOT READ THIS
BOOK FROM
BEGINNING TO END!

You can't believe you wasted your allowance on Vampire in a Can. It's the dumbest Halloween costume ever made. But wait. Don't throw away the can! There's something else in there. A packet — labeled DANGER. . . .

Do you dare open the packet — or not? Either way, you're in *grave* trouble. What do you do when you start turning into a vampire? Is there a cure for being undead? What happens when your best friend starts looking like your next meal? How does a vampire deal with braces? And how do you protect yourself from a vampire dog?

This scary adventure is all about you. You decide what will happen. And you decide how terrifying the scares will be!

Start on Page 1. Then follow the instructions at the bottom of each page. *You* make the choices. If you choose well, you'll survive this adventure. But if you make the wrong choice . . . BEWARE!

SO TAKE A DEEP BREATH. CROSS YOUR FINGERS. AND TURN TO PAGE 1 TO *GIVE YOURSELF GOOSEBUMPS*!

READER BEWARE —
YOU CHOOSE THE SCARE!

Look for more
GIVE YOURSELF GOOSEBUMPS adventures
from R.L. STINE

R.L. STINE
GIVE YOURSELF

Goosebumps®

PLEASE DON'T FEED
THE VAMPIRE!

AN
APPLE
PAPERBACK

SCHOLASTIC INC.
New York Toronto London Auckland Sydney

A PARACHUTE PRESS BOOK

ISBN 0-590-93477-5

12 11 10 9 8 7 6 5 4 3 2 1   7 8 9/9 0 1 2/0

Printed in the U.S.A.   40

First Scholastic printing, March 1997

"I look like a nerd, don't I? Like a complete nerd," you moan to your friend Gabe. In the mirror you see your costume and wince. "Halloween is only a few days away. I'm doomed!"

You and Gabe have been best friends for two years. Gabe has long brown hair, wire-rimmed glasses — and a way of giving advice that sometimes bugs you.

"You do look pretty stupid," Gabe admits. "Where did you get that costume, anyway?"

"It's called Vampire in a Can," you explain, holding up the cardboard can. "I bought it from Mr. Reuterly at Scary Stuff."

"I don't believe it!" Gabe slaps his forehead. "You bought a costume from the Eyeball Man? What if he took out his glass eye — right there in the store — and *showed* it to you?"

"He never takes out his glass eye," you answer.

"Okay, okay," Gabe says. "But your costume is still ridiculous. It's just a set of plastic fangs, a cheap little black cape, and a fake tattoo of fang marks for your neck. Isn't there anything else in the can?"

You pick it up and peer inside. "Hey, look!" you cry.

Go on to PAGE 2.

2

"What?" Gabe asks, looking interested.

"There *is* something else in the can," you answer. You reach in and pull out a small plastic packet that was stuck to the inside. It looks like a ketchup packet.

"What is it?" Gabe moves closer.

"I think it's fake blood," you tell him.

"Really? Cool," Gabe says. He picks up the Vampire in a Can box and reads the label. "That's weird. It doesn't say anything on the box about fake blood."

Then you notice the writing on the packet.

In bloodred letters, it says DANGER — KEEP AWAY.

You hand the packet to Gabe. He reads the label and his eyes grow wide. "Are you going to open it?" he asks.

You gulp. The words on the packet are kind of scary.

But you're *dying* to know what's inside.

So? Are you going to open it?

If you open the packet, turn to PAGE 34.
If you don't open it, turn to PAGE 67.

"Yeow!" you cry, jerking away from the vicious dog.

But Buttermilk is fast. He lunges at you, baring long, sharp fangs. His hot breath stinks.

Oh, no. He's a vampire dog too!

"Get off, Buttermilk!" you command. You push him away and scramble to your feet.

Buttermilk lunges at you!

"Yikes!" you shout. You dash across the Berklines' yard and jump the fence. You run around to the back.

There, on the back patio, are three more dogs. All bitten in the neck. All changing into vampire dogs!

Two of them are dachshunds. The third is a big mutt. They lift their heads and sniff the air.

Then they all howl and leap at you!

You race to the gate. Then skid to a stop.

Buttermilk is waiting just outside the fence!

Turn to PAGE 20.

4

Standing in the doorway are the vampires. All of them!

Countess Yvonne stalks toward you. Right behind her are at least twenty others. Hungry for blood!

"Don't be afraid," Countess Yvonne says. "We only want to drain the rest of your fresh, human blood. Then you'll truly be one of us. Don't worry. It won't hurt."

The last person who told you that was your dentist.

"Run!" you shout at Gabe.

But you can't run. The vampires are pushing into the small room, filling the doorway.

You feel like you're losing your mind. You cry, "I'm going batty!"

The countess stops in her tracks and starts laughing. "'Batty'! What a hoot!" The other vampires begin laughing uncontrollably. The corny pun has them in hysterics!

The bloodsuckers are distracted. Here's your chance! You drop to your hands and knees and start crawling. Gabe follows you. You scramble like mad between the legs of the guffawing vampires.

Quick, make a decision. Which way now?

If you run back the way you came, turn to PAGE 18.

If you try to find the Garlic Spray, turn to PAGE 56.

The red liquid gleams. A vampire places a plastic straw in one of the goblets and holds it toward you. "Sip?"

You lick your dry lips.

You'd die for a gulp.

But you swallow hard and shake your head.

You can't let yourself drink it. If you do, and it's blood — and you *know* it's blood — you're pretty sure you'll be a vampire forever. And forever is a long time.

"No," you repeat. "I'll pass on the blood!"

"I'm sorry you feel that way," Countess Yvonne says.

She gives one short nod to the others. They glide toward you. Closing in on you.

In desperation, you search for a weapon. But the only thing you see are the goblets of blood.

Frantically, you dart to the table and lift a goblet. You toss the whole glassful of liquid into the countess's face!

Turn to PAGE 16.

You back up, heart pounding in fear.

What now? Is Gabe a vampire too? Did Fifi bite him?

Gabe bursts out laughing. "Ha-ha. Got you good!" he says, doubling over.

"You creep!" you yell.

Gabe laughs again, then tells you the truth. "It was easy," he says. "I just ran over to the Eyeball Man's store. I remembered seeing something there called Dog in a Can. So I bought a bunch of them. Sure enough, there were these little packets inside. They said, 'Danger — Keep Away' — just like on the blood packet. So I opened one, and it was a dog biscuit. I figured it was worth a try."

"You mean you gave the biscuits to the vampire dogs, and they changed back?" you gasp. "Excellent!"

Then an idea hits you. A great idea!

"Do you have one of those special dog biscuits left?" you ask.

"Yeah," Gabe replies. "So what?"

"Give me one," you say. "I think I want to be a dog for Halloween!"

THE END

You're terrified of the dog. Then you remember. Fido can't kill you.

You're a vampire! Only a few things can kill you.

A stake through the heart. Being exposed to sunlight. Being burned alive.

You bare your fangs and hiss. The Doberman slinks away, whining.

"Not bad," Gabe admits.

Oh, by the way. There's one other thing that can knock you out. . . .

A blood shortage.

Without blood, vampires don't die. But they become so weak, they can't move.

That's what's happening to you now. With a moan, you collapse.

Uh-oh. Turn to PAGE 36.

8

You want to change back into a kid. But you don't have a clue how.

So you fly back out the window, searching for Gabe.

Your radar spots him. You dart down and land gently on his shoulder.

Gabe twists around and stares into your tiny bat face.

"Yuck!" he says. "You're ugly. Can't you change back?"

You just sit there, screeching.

Finally Gabe nods in understanding. "I guess I'll have to take you home and keep you as a pet. Boy, my mom is going to freak. Maybe I can figure out a cure someday."

Unfortunately, Gabe never figures it out. He does, however, grow up to become a major league baseball player. As a private joke, he lets you live in the clubhouse — as the unofficial *bat* boy!

THE END

"I think I'll go for choice number three," you tell Gabe. "I'm tired. Maybe if I take a nap, this whole vampire thing will wear off."

"Yeah." Gabe nods. But he looks nervous.

You can tell he's wondering: What if it doesn't wear off?

You're wondering about that too.

You scribble a note to your parents. It says that you're sick and have gone to bed. Then you send Gabe home.

You curl up in your bed for a long nap.

When you open your eyes, it's ten o'clock at night — and you're thirstier than ever.

You race to the mirror hanging on your closet door.

Nothing. No reflection. You're not there.

"I've got to have blood!" you say out loud.

Go on to PAGE 30.

This has gone too far, you decide.

You've got to get help from some adults — and fast.

Before the vampires bite Gabe!

You race out of the office and run all the way home. But when you reach your house, you get a sinking feeling.

There are no lights on inside the house. No cars in the driveway.

Your parents aren't home.

Weird, you think. They didn't have any plans to go out.

You feel a sudden chill up your spine.

Slowly, you walk up your front steps and open the door.

Turn to PAGE 131.

You don't trust the old vampire woman. The minute you're free, you shove her into the cell and slam the door! Then you turn the black iron key in the lock.

"Oh, what fools! What fools!" the old woman cries.

She's right, of course. You are fools.

You're in a dungeon full of bloodsucking vampires! How do you *ever* hope to get out unless you trust someone? At least you could put your faith in a sweet little old lady!

True — she's a sweet little old lady *with fangs*.

But who else is going to help you?

There's very little hope now. You shouldn't even bother to go on with this book.

That is, unless you can pass a test to prove that you have good sense.

Turn to PAGE 132 to take the test.

12

Walking to the front of the building, you complain, "I'm dying of thirst."

"Quit talking about death," orders Gabe.

There's a buzzer outside the office. Gabe pushes it.

Instantly, the office door swings open. A light comes on inside.

You peer in and see a small waiting room. At the back is another door. The sign on the second door says NO ADMITTANCE.

But there's no one in the office.

"Who opened the door?" you wonder.

Gabe whispers, "If this were a movie, I'd be screaming, '*Don't go inside, dummy!*'"

You must be a dummy. You step inside.

Turn to PAGE 24.

Before the parrot reaches you, a net scoops him up. The net is attached to a pole. A pole held by Mr. Weniger.

"Got him!" Weniger declares triumphantly.

He pops the squawking bird into a cage.

"What's going on?" you demand.

"I'll show you," he offers. "Come with me."

You follow Weniger outside. In his driveway is a large van. Inside it is a menagerie of vampire pets!

"I've rounded up all the vampire animals," he announces proudly. "Letting Fifi become a vampire was almost a disaster. She could have started an epidemic. Vampirism could have spread across the entire world!"

That *would* be bad. "But you got them all?" you ask.

"Every last one," Weniger replies confidently.

"What are you going to do with the animals?" you ask.

"Sell them to the circus," he explains. "I'm going to make my fortune!"

"So this is a happy ending," you say. You slap at a pesky mosquito that just bit your neck.

A pesky *vampire* mosquito . . .

THE END

14

When you wake up a couple of hours later, the sun has set. A shiver of excitement runs down your spine.

You climb out your bedroom window and slip into the night. This will be a blast, you think. Vampires rule!

You slink through the neighborhood. Rats and mice meekly approach you. You are their master. "Cool," you whisper to yourself. "I'm king of the rodents."

Who will be your first victim?

You'll find her name on PAGE 48.

You race to answer the phone.

"Hello?"

It's your mom. "Hi, sweetie," she says casually. "Listen, I need you to do something for me."

"Uh, hi, Mom," you say. "Listen, I can't right now. I've got to run after Fifi. She just got loose!"

"That's okay," your mom answers. "She'll come back. Now here's what I want you to buy at the store. . . . "

By the time you're done listening to her, ten minutes have passed. You and Gabe run out into the street.

Fifi is gone!

Turn to PAGE 75.

16

"You wretch!" the countess screams. "What have you done?" Her terror-filled voice stuns you.

Blood splashes across her face and runs down her neck.

It's just blood, you think. Isn't that what she drinks?

But you quickly understand. The sight of blood has driven the other vampires into a frenzy.

They rush over to her and attack — by licking her face! They slobber at her cheeks, her neck, her eyes and nose.

The countess screams, sinking to the floor.

Are they going to eat her? Your stomach turns. You feel faint.

And worst of all, you feel thirsty. Part of you wants to join them — to lick up the blood too!

No, you tell yourself. Now's your chance to get away!

If you want to escape from this place, turn to PAGE 79.

If you want to lick up the blood, turn to PAGE 110.

"Okay," you agree. You shake Reuterly's hand. "I'll do it."

He rubs his hands together. "Good. Let's go."

Holding you, Reuterly spreads his cape like bat wings. As if by magic, the two of you float straight out of the grave. You land among the cemetery's gravestones.

"Wow!" you gush, amazed. "Can you teach me that trick?"

"Later," Reuterly answers. "Now lead me to your young friends. I'm quite thirsty. Who will it be?"

That's easy. Robbie Morgan.

Robbie's three years older than you, and he lives on your block. He's always grabbing your bike. He calls you "Rat Face" in front of your friends.

"I know just the guy," you tell Mr. Reuterly.

"Excellent," Mr. Reuterly declares. "Lead the way."

Turn to PAGE 42.

Run! you think. And don't look back!

You retrace your steps. Past the coffins. Past the table of blood-filled goblets. You finally reach the room you fell into from the trapdoor.

You dash in and slam the door. The darkness is total.

CLICK! You hear Gabe slide the bolt shut.

SHUFFLE! SHUFFLE!

"What's that noise?" you whisper.

A weird, quavery voice speaks out of the dark. "It is I, Count von Smelling. The greatest vampire of them all!"

Oh, great! You escaped from the other vampires — but now you're locked in a room with the big cheese! You can't see him, but you can imagine how Count von Smelling must look. Ten feet tall. Burning red eyes. Six-inch fangs.

You're finished!

Or . . . are you? Turn to PAGE 38.

You pop your head out the bathroom door.

"If I get some sleep, I'll be okay," you tell your mom.

"Okay, honey," she answers. She blows you a kiss. "See you in the morning."

When you wake up the next day, you tell your mother you're still sick.

She believes you. After all, the color seems to have drained out of your skin.

"Be sure to drink lots of liquids," your mom calls as she hurries off to work.

"Don't worry," you call back. "That's just what I had in mind."

Turn to PAGE 62.

The vampire dogs close in on you. A small set of teeth clamps down on your leg.

"Hey, get off me!" you yell.

You jerk your leg so hard, the dachshund goes flying. He lands with a splash in a kiddie wading pool.

For an instant, the other two dogs look away, surprised.

It gives you time to glance around quickly. Looking for escape routes.

There's a door leading from the patio into the garage. If you hurry, you might be able to hide in the garage before the dogs get you.

But you might be trapped in there.

Or you can make a dash for the house. But what if the sliding-glass doors are locked?

Well? Do something — fast!

If you dash to the garage, turn to PAGE 136.
If you run into the house, turn to PAGE 93.

You hope your mom has a strong heart. You open wide and say, "Ahhh."

Your mom peers in. "What's happened to your canine teeth?" she asks, eyes growing wide. "They're so sharp! Are they bothering you?"

Hey, if you can't tell your mom you're undead, who *can* you tell? "Oh, Mom," you moan. "I bought this costume called Vampire in a Can and there was a packet of something inside — I think it was blood — and I drank it! And now I've turned into a vampire!"

"Don't worry." Your mom gives you a comforting pat on the back. "I know what to do. Stay here. I'll be right back."

Turn to PAGE 63.

"Wait," the countess calls. Her face looms over the coffin. "I promised to answer all your questions."

Groggy, you manage to ask, "Why?"

"That Vampire in a Can idea was a mistake," the countess explains. "You see, we thought we needed some 'young blood.' But you kid vampires! You're *too* good at finding victims. Soon, there'll be more vampires than humans. So I've decided to put the young ones on ice. Don't worry, though. You'll have your turn — one day."

"Gabe?" you mumble as if calling his name in a dream.

"Oh, Gabe?" the countess explains. "We drank his blood. He's in the coffin next to yours. Now, sleep tight, dear." She laughs a silvery laugh. "And don't let the coffin-bugs bite!"

THE END

The minute you see Robbie's parents in the driveway, you panic and run.

Down the steps. Across the front lawn. Into the street.

You run all the way to the park at the end of the street. Then you hide in the bushes.

RRRREEEE! RREEE! RREEE! RREEE!

A police siren pierces the stillness of the night.

Uh-oh. That's right. You forgot!

Robbie Morgan's dad is a police officer!

Then you hear Mr. Morgan's voice on his police loudspeaker. He's calling your name!

You've been recognized!

Run to PAGE 121.

CLICK! CLICK! CLACK!

"What's that sound?" you whisper.

"It's my knees knocking," Gabe explains. "This place is terminally creepy. Let's just book home, tell your parents the whole story, and let them deal with it."

"No way!" you declare. "I'm staying till I get what I came for."

As you bicker, the back door opens. A short, pudgy man walks into the office.

"Well, well," he says, giving you a fatherly smile. He doesn't look scary at all. "You must be the one who called. About Vampire in a Can?"

You nod and start to answer, but he keeps talking.

"Fine. Glad you found us so easily. I'm Herman Carmine. Come with me," he says, jerking his head toward the NO ADMITTANCE door. "We'll fix you up in no time."

Gabe steps forward.

"Not *you*," the man says firmly to Gabe. "*You* stay here."

Turn to PAGE 60.

Fifi is sitting up in the seat, watching Dracula on the big screen.

You twist out of the manager's grip and run up the aisle, stopping at your pooch's row.

"Fifi," you call softly. "Come here, girl."

"Shhhh!" Everyone in the row turns to shush you.

That is, everyone but Fifi. She's staring, transfixed, at the movie screen.

"Fifi!" you cry, grabbing her collar.

Your dog looks you in the eye, coldly, as if you're a stranger. Then she bares her teeth and leaps at you!

You scream!

"Quit screaming!" yells an angry moviegoer.

As Fifi bites into your throat, you think: Where's the manager now — when you really need him?

Quiet! Stop screaming and turn to PAGE 105.

"I say we go back to Mr. Reuterly," you tell Gabe. "Maybe he knows what was in that packet of —"

"Don't say it," Gabe interrupts. "Let's just go."

You nod and stuff the costume back into the Vampire in a Can can.

You head for the kitchen door. Gabe pulls it open. A beam of daylight streams in.

"Hold it!" you scream.

You cringe, shielding your eyes from the light. You double over in burning pain. In a few seconds you'll be as crispy as a french fry!

"Close the door — quick!" you shout at Gabe. "The light is killing me!"

Turn to PAGE 54.

"Okay, okay," you agree. "Who are you? Where do you live?"

"This is Jeremy Weniger," he snarls. "I'm over on Mulberry Street."

Jeremy Weniger? The weirdo? The guy who keeps caged cockroaches as pets?

"Hurry up," he continues, "or I might do something *you'll* regret."

He chuckles softly to himself. Then he hangs up.

"Oh, brother," you moan. "Fifi is over at Mr. Weniger's house!"

"Yikes!" Gabe replies. "The guy who never mows his lawn? The one with the weird gargoyle on his mailbox? The one who stays up all night and never goes out?"

"Yeah," you nod. "We'd better get over there before Fifi bites him."

"Or before Weniger bites Fifi!" Gabe adds, heading for the door.

Turn to PAGE 111.

"I'm drinking the Garlic Spray," you tell Gabe. "I really think you should too."

"Okay, but you go first," Gabe says slyly.

Each of you pours one bottle of Garlic Spray into a glass. You chug-a-lug yours.

"P-U," Gabe complains. "Your breath is killing me!"

"It probably will," you retort, "unless you drink yours too. Now!"

Gabe gulps his down. Pretty soon, the whole room stinks of garlic. It smells so bad, your mom comes barging in to see what's wrong.

"What's going on in here?" she asks, holding her nose. "You smell like that creepy man who owns Scary Stuff. What's his name? Mr. Reuterly."

How can that be? you wonder.

Mr. Reuterly wouldn't use garlic. He's a vampire!

"Yes," your mom goes on. "He used to eat garlic all the time. He told me it was to ward off vampires. Can you imagine? Then, a few months ago, he suddenly stopped."

Turn to PAGE 133.

Slowly, you turn to see who's behind you.

"Good evening," a dark, shadowy figure whispers. "I see you've found my home-away-from-home."

The shadowy figure steps forward. A beam of moonlight strikes his face. Then his fangs. Then the glass eye sitting on his palm!

"Mr. Reuterly!" you cry.

Go on to PAGE 112.

"Honey? Are you awake?" a voice calls from the hallway.

Uh-oh. Mom!

"Uh, yeah, I'm up. But I'm still not feeling too well," you call back.

Your mom pushes open your door and comes in.

"Should I take your temperature?" she asks, sounding worried. "Here — open your mouth and let me look at your tongue."

Yikes! You don't want your mom to see your fangs!

Or do you? Maybe she can help. . . .

If you want to show your mom the fangs, turn to PAGE 21.

If not, turn to PAGE 78.

"What do you mean I'll make mistakes?" you demand.

"Oh, you know." Reuterly shrugs. "You'll get careless about who you bite and when. Someone will see you, and pretty soon the whole town will be hunting you down. The next thing you know, they'll be trying to drive a stake through your heart. Being undead is no picnic, believe me."

Whoa! you think. He's right. There's a lot you don't know about being a vampire.

"Maybe having a teacher isn't a bad idea," you say.

"And all you have to do is find me young victims." Reuterly holds out his hand. "So? Do we have a deal?"

If you agree to his terms, turn to PAGE 17.
If not, turn to PAGE 52.

Right now, your future looks dark. Like this cell. But don't panic! Just find the book. And the match.

"Where's the table?" whispers Gabe.

You feel a sharp pain. "Yeow! I just bumped into it."

"Good work," Gabe laughs.

You feel for the match on the tabletop. A splinter pierces your finger.

Gabe smells the blood seeping from your wound. He grabs your hand and licks it. You pull your hand away.

"Type O Positive. My favorite flavor," Gabe murmurs, smacking his lips.

"Quit it," you order. "Let's get busy!"

At last you find the match and the ancient, leather-bound book. You open it to the page marked with the ribbon.

You strike the match. In its flare you read old-fashioned lettering. It says:

TO REVERSE VAMPIRISM —

But the rest of the page is torn out!

Turn to PAGE 81.

First you sink your teeth into Gabe's throat.

Then he bites you back!

Uh-oh, you think. This wasn't part of the plan. . . .

Within seconds, both of you feel a strange change. Your fangs grow longer. Your skin turns pale.

You're both full-fledged vampires!

There's no changing back. The transformation is complete!

"Whoops," Gabe says sheepishly. "I guess that wasn't the right cure."

Nope. But now that you're a vampire, you might as well make the best of it.

"I know what to do," you announce with a toothy grin. "Let's go to the local blood bank and make a big withdrawal!"

THE END

"Yeah," you tell Gabe. "I'll open it. Give it back."

"Be careful," Gabe warns. "You don't want to squirt that gunk all over your cute little cape."

"Thanks, jokeboy," you grumble.

First you try to rip open the packet with your fingernails. But the plastic won't tear.

Frustrated, you pull the fake fangs out of your mouth. Then you put the packet between your teeth and yank hard.

A syrupy liquid shoots out, spilling into your mouth. A tiny bit dribbles out, leaving a red streak on your chin.

"Ummm. Yum!" you say, slurping up the liquid. It's so good, you want to drink every drop. Quickly, you squeeze the rest of the packet into your mouth.

"What *is* that stuff?" Gabe asks, squinting at you.

"It definitely isn't ketchup," you reply. "But it's excellent. I love it!"

"It's gross," Gabe declares, scowling. "It looks like blood. Real blood."

"Blood?" you cry.

Turn to PAGE 50.

"Mr. Reuterly!" you cry.

You always kind of liked Mr. Reuterly. Even though he's the Eyeball Man. For a moment, you hesitate. But when you see his fangs, you know what you must do.

You aim the plastic bottle of Garlic Spray at his face and start pumping the spray button.

"Take that, sucker!" you yell. The smell of garlic makes you want to puke.

A fine spray of liquid hits Reuterly in his eyes.

"Oowww!" he screams, doubling over in pain.

The other vampires don't want any part of your garlic gun. You hear them moan and gag from the garlic as they scurry down the stairs.

You and Gabe high-five each other. Then you each grab two bottles of Garlic Spray and dash toward the exit.

You don't stop running until you get home.

Gabe collapses on the floor in your room.

"Phew!" he pants. "Close one!"

"Yeah," you agree. "But it's not over yet. We're still vampires!"

Turn to PAGE 115.

36

Gabe lifts you to your feet. You barely make it to Scary Stuff. The front door is locked.

But Gabe finds an unlocked window on the side street. He pushes it up and climbs inside. You follow.

Gabe quickly locates the shelf full of Vampire in a Can costumes. Eagerly, you pry open the lid of one can. You frantically feel around for the small packet of lifesaving liquid. Your mouth is foaming!

Blood! Give me blood!

You're going to pass out again if you don't have it. Right this second!

Stay awake till you get to PAGE 57.

As it swoops toward your face, you bat the screeching bird to the ground.

At once, it flies up again. It darts at your neck.

"Help!" you shriek.

A door opens near the back of the house. Then you hear the clicking sound of claws on wood.

Batting the parrot away, you glance toward the hallway. Good grief! A dozen vampire pets are racing toward you.

Cats — with fangs. Puppies — with fangs. Mice, snakes, rabbits, tarantulas, hamsters. With fangs!

You try to run out of the house, but you trip over the doormat. *WHAM!* You hit the ground hard.

Instantly, the vampire pets are on you, biting you. Draining your blood.

"Helllp!" you cry, flailing at them.

Another door opens. More claws on wood. Your heart sinks as you realize: Another dog is coming.

And this one sounds huge!

Turn to PAGE 135.

We've had it, you think. Count von Smelling is going to drain all our blood!

Then Gabe speaks up.

"Excuse me," he says. "But exactly *what* makes you the greatest vampire of all time?"

"I am the oldest," Count von Smelling answers proudly. "I am in the *Guinness Book of World Records!*"

That's what makes him the greatest?

"Uh . . . congratulations," you say politely.

"Wow, you must have seen it all," Gabe adds.

"Oh, I have," Count von Smelling agrees eagerly. "It all started back in the year 1327. That's B.C., of course . . . "

The count starts to tell you his life story. And it's some long story! You quickly realize why the other vampires keep him in here. His quavery voice drones on, hour after hour. Day after day. Year after year.

You've heard the expression "bored to death"?

Unfortunately, you and Gabe are now among the undead. But during the eternity you spend with Count von Smelling, you never stop hoping. . . .

THE END

Gabe whistles. "Calls accepted after dark only. That's weird. Are you going to phone?"

Staring at Gabe's neck, your thirst returns. The thirst for . . .

You think, *don't think of blood.*

Too late! You just thought of it!

"What choice do I have?" you moan, and hurry to a pay phone on the corner.

You pick up the receiver and punch in the number.

It rings thirteen times before a man's voice answers.

"Thank you for calling Vampire in a Can," the voice says. "How can I help you?"

Quickly you explain your problem.

"Yessss," the man says in a slithery tone. "You must come to 999 Sanguine Road. We'll be here till midnight."

Then he hangs up.

"*Sanguine* Road?" Gabe exclaims when you tell him the address. "I know that word. 'Sanguine' means 'bloody'! Stay away from there, I'm telling you. Don't go!"

If you take Gabe's advice, turn to PAGE 70.
If you ignore Gabe, turn to PAGE 91.

40

You jump into some prickly bushes to avoid being hit by Weniger's car.

Meanwhile, he roars off.

"Come on!" you yell. "Let's follow that lunatic!"

You and Gabe run after the car as fast as you can. Luckily, Weniger hits a red light, so you catch up.

Then he loses you again. He turns the corner and zooms down the road to a small shopping center. There are six stores on one end, a movie theater in the middle, and some offices on the other end.

You spot Weniger's car in the parking lot — but he and the dog crate are gone.

You scan the stores, trying to guess where he went.

"He could be anywhere," Gabe moans.

You point. "Look — there's a pet store on the end. I bet he went in there."

"Maybe," Gabe says. "But what about the movies? They're showing *Dracula's Bloodiest Revenge*."

If you think he went into the pet store, turn to PAGE 109.

If you think he went into the movie, turn to PAGE 59.

"Forget the phone!" you shout. "We've got to catch Fifi. Come on!"

You dash out the kitchen door and down the steps, chasing your crazy dog. But Gabe doesn't follow.

"I've got to answer the phone!" Gabe calls after you. "It might be my mom. She said she'd call."

"Okay," you shout. "I'll be back as soon as I can."

Fifi is already way ahead of you. You see her about five houses away, darting into a neighbor's yard.

When you get to the yard, you stop. And stare, amazed at what's lying on the grass.

"Buttermilk?" you call softly. It's the big golden retriever that belongs to the Berklines!

The fuzzy yellow dog is on his side. Motionless. But that's not what scares you.

What scares you are the two little bite marks on his neck — streaked with blood!

Turn to PAGE 102.

42

Slinking through your neighborhood, you glance nervously at the cars that pass by.

You feel paranoid. Can people tell you're vampires?

"Don't act so suspiciously," Mr. Reuterly advises you. "That's my first tip. See? I told you you needed my help."

Don't act suspiciously? you think. Well, duhhh!

"And never smile at anyone — unless you plan to bite them," he goes on. "People feel uneasy when they see fangs."

Oh, brother! You roll your eyes. More hot news! A minute later, you arrive at Robbie Morgan's house. "This is it," you tell Reuterly. "What should I do?"

"Nothing," he answers. He glances at the house, then the garage. "Lights on in the house. But no cars in the driveway. Perfect! His parents must not be home."

Mr. Reuterly goes up to the door and rings the bell. The door opens — and Gabe steps out!

Before you can warn him, Reuterly grabs Gabe by the shoulders and bites his neck!

Turn to PAGE 69.

An upstairs light flips on.

"Who's there?" Gabe whispers through a big hole in the window.

"It's me!" you whisper back. "Hurry! I need help."

A minute later, Gabe comes out the backdoor into his backyard.

"You've got to help me," you beg him. "I bit my own dad on the neck — I couldn't help it. I need blood. But my dad put braces on me. I can't really bite anything."

Gabe paces back and forth on his patio. Finally he comes up with an idea. "Let's go to Mr. Reuterly's store, Scary Stuff. We'll buy some more of those Vampire in a Can things. Then you can drink the packets from all the cans. Maybe that'll do the trick."

"Maybe," you say. You squint at your watch. "But it's awfully late. What if the store is closed?"

"Then we'll go back in the morning," Gabe answers.

"No way," you reply. "I can't wait till morning. I need blood now. Got any other ideas?"

"Yeah," Gabe says. "How about a piece of raw steak?"

If you go to Scary Stuff tonight, turn to PAGE 114.

If you'd rather eat raw steak, turn to PAGE 122.

"We'll follow the bats!" you snap.

With a shudder, you realize you'd rather hang out with bats than with Gabe.

"Come on," you command, hurrying to the back of the factory.

"You seem to know where you're going," Gabe says, trying to keep up with you.

Somehow, you do know. You're following some kind of inner radar — like a bat. And your radar tells you there's a door in the back of this place.

"We're getting closer to the bats," you tell Gabe.

Gabe puffs, "You act like you want to *party* with those bats or something! Don't you want to be normal?"

Normal? What's normal?

You start running faster.

Turn to PAGE 89.

"I say we go with plan two," you tell Gabe. "We do research. Maybe we can find a cure that way."

"Great!" Gabe declares. "I'll go to the video store and rent every vampire movie I can find. Be right back."

But by the time Gabe returns, you're feeling weaker — and thirstier — than ever.

"Hurry," you whimper. "Put in a tape."

Gabe pops in a tape. He pushes the button and *Dracula's Excellent Adventure* starts.

Big mistake.

Right off the bat, Dracula turns into a bat. He flies through a window and bites a woman on the neck. Now you've really worked up a thirst!

"I need blood!" you cry, jumping up and flapping your arms like a big, goofy bat.

Turn to PAGE 88.

"Yes!" you shout. There's a cellular phone inside the car! You slide into the front seat.

Fingers shaking, you dial your home phone number.

It rings six times. Finally Gabe answers.

"Listen," you spit out. "I'm trapped in the garage of the green house down the street. Come help me!"

"Why are you trapped?" Gabe asks.

"Because of the vampire dogs!" you cry. "Fifi bit all the dogs in the neighborhood. She turned them into crazed vampires. And now they've got me cornered."

"And you want *me* to come risk my life?" Gabe demands. "Later, dude."

"Wait!" you plead. "There's got to be something you can do."

"Yeah. I can call the dogcatcher!" Gabe says firmly.

"No!" you shriek. "I don't want them to catch Fifi. If they see her fangs, they'll . . . they'll put her to sleep."

"Leave it to me," Gabe orders, hanging up the phone.

Uh-oh. What is Mr. Know-it-all going to do?

Turn to PAGE 118.

"Dog therapy! What a dumb idea!" Gabe mutters.

"What about those red puncture marks on your neck?" you ask Weniger.

"Oh, this? I, uh, accidentally stabbed myself with my fork while eating spaghetti," he explains.

"Smooth move," Gabe scoffs.

"Yes, well — I've got to be going. Hope you catch up with your dog," Weniger mumbles. Then he hurries away across the parking lot.

You aren't paying attention. A strange feeling is coming over you. A transformation . . .

It's as if Fifi's bite turned you into . . . something inhuman.

"You look really pale," Gabe says, sounding worried.

Yeah, you think. I need to put a little color in my cheeks — the color red!

You feel the strongest urge to bite someone.

Don't bite anyone until you turn to PAGE 86.

48

You reach nasty old Mrs. Winesap's house. You ring her bell. The door opens. "Who's bothering me at dinnertime?" she demands crossly.

You open your mouth wide. Time for revenge!

Then the smell hits you. Mrs. Winesap has been eating garlic bread. Garlic! The downfall of all vampires! The reek makes you dizzy.

"If you're here to get your silly Frisbee back, you can forget about it!" Mrs. Winesap snaps. She slams the door in your face.

You sit on her doorstep, heaving.

Turn to PAGE 85.

Drink the red liquid in one of those goblets?

You think: *Rule one: Never take candy from strangers. Rule two: Never take blood from strange vampires.*

But you suspect that the liquid in those goblets will *really* quench your thirst.

"All right," you agree, walking to the table.

You lift a silver goblet to your lips. You swig it down. But it tastes terrible.

"Yuck!" you exclaim. "That's not blood! What is it?"

"Vampire medicine," the countess replies. "To keep you well while you're asleep. Asleep for a hundred years!"

She leans toward you. "Sleep," she coos. "Sleep."

You stare into her eyes. Oooohh! You feel so heavy. So drowsy. . . .

The countess is hypnotizing you!

Your legs wobble. Then you slip to the ground. A vampire carries you to a black coffin. He lays you in it.

"Sleep, my friend," he murmurs and reaches for the coffin lid.

Turn to PAGE 22.

"No way that's blood!" you say with a nervous laugh.

But your heart starts beating a little faster. Could it be? You remember scraping your hand last week and licking the wound. This stuff tastes the same.

Maybe. But right now you've got something else on your mind.

"I'm thirsty," you declare, rushing to the kitchen. "I've got to get a drink."

Gabe follows you, talking a mile a minute.

"If you didn't swallow, spit it out," he orders. "Gargle with mouthwash. Or maybe brush with peroxide toothpaste! Or do both!"

"Water," you groan. "I'm so thirsty! I need water."

You stick your mouth under the faucet to gulp from the tap. But as the water hits your tongue, you jerk away.

"Yuck!" you exclaim. "That tastes terrible."

"I thought you were thirsty," Gabe says, eyeing you strangely.

"I am," you tell him. "But not for water. For . . . something else."

To find out what for, turn to PAGE 58.

"I told you it was a trap," Gabe complains. "Now we're both vampires. And we'll never change back."

"I don't believe it," you tell him. "There must be some way to change back. There's got to be!"

Gabe shakes his head. "The vampire who bit me told me there wasn't," he says. "But —" He breaks off.

"But what?" you urge.

"When he was taking me here, we passed by a sign on the wall that said 'Midnight Shift — Keep Away. Danger.' Under the sign was a shelf full of plastic bottles. The labels on them said 'Garlic Spray.'"

"Garlic?" You frown. "In olden days, people wore garlic around their necks to keep vampires away."

"I know. Look, could you get me out of these things?" Gabe asks. He nods at the cuffs on his hands and feet.

You look around for a key. But you hear footsteps.

You whirl around just as a frail, gray-haired old lady appears at the door.

"Aha!" she croaks. "So there you are!"

Turn to PAGE 66.

"No!" you shout at Mr. Reuterly. "No way! I won't help you attack my friends. Now let me go!"

You try to push him away. But he's too strong.

"Well, then," he snarls, "you leave me no choice. Perhaps you're not as stale and lifeless as the other vampires I know. Perhaps because you're young. . . ."

In a flash, he exposes his long, sharp fangs. Then he sinks them into your flesh!

Turn to PAGE 74.

You reach out and ring the doorbell.

"Push it again!" orders Gabe. "Keep ringing until Weniger comes back!"

You push the bell again. *DING-DONG*.

You hear a door slam. An outside door.

Then footsteps.

"Hey," you whisper to Gabe. "I think he's sneaking out the back."

Gabe leaps off the porch, and you follow him. At the back of the house, you peek into the garage.

Mr. Weniger is loading a dog crate into the trunk of an old station wagon.

Is Fifi inside?

"Wait!" you call out, running up to the car. "Mr. Weniger! My dog!"

Weniger ignores you. He jumps behind the wheel, starts the engine, and backs out — really fast.

The car zooms right at you!

Turn to PAGE 40.

Gabe slams shut the door and rushes over to you.

You fan your face. It feels as if you got a mega sunburn.

Finally, the pain goes away.

"What happened?" Gabe asks.

"The light," you answer. "Haven't you ever seen a Dracula movie? Vampires can't go outside in daylight."

"Not even with sunblock on?" Gabe jokes.

"Hey, wise guy, you want to be my lunchtime beverage?" you snap.

"Sorry," murmurs Gabe. "So now what?"

"Now we wait," you reply grimly.

Luckily, it's October, so it gets dark early. You and Gabe hike to Scary Stuff, Mr. Reuterly's store.

A block from the store, Gabe grabs your arm. "Look!" he shouts. "It's the Eyeball Man. He's locking the door!"

Hurry to PAGE 76.

"Don't be stupid," you tell Gabe. "It's not Weniger in a dress. I meant, that must be his mother. Mrs. Weniger."

You don't know why they took Fifi. But the Wenigers won't get away with stealing your dog!

The next day, you and Gabe bike over to the pet store bright and early. The old woman is just opening up.

You lock up your bikes and hurry through the front door.

"What the —?" Gabe's mouth drops open.

Every single animal is gone.

Every cage empty.

The entire pet store is completely cleaned out!

Turn to PAGE 71.

56

"Where was that Garlic Spray?" you shout at Gabe.

Without answering, he sprints down the hallway. At the end, you spot a staircase that leads up to the warehouse.

The two of you clamber up the steps. The vampires are in hot pursuit.

The warehouse is jammed with all kinds of vampire costumes and products. But finally you find the sign on the wall. The one Gabe told you about. MIDNIGHT SHIFT — KEEP AWAY. DANGER.

Beneath it are plastic bottles of Garlic Spray.

Desperately, you grab one of the bottles and flick off the cap. You whirl around — just as a balding vampire lunges at you. As he draws near, you realize: You *know* this vampire!

Turn to PAGE 35 to see who it is.

Where is it? Where's the packet of blood?

"This one doesn't have any," you cry weakly.

You grab another can and rip the lid off. No packet.

"Help me look!" you command Gabe.

But not a single can holds that precious red packet.

"Gabe," you whisper softly. "I — I —"

But those are your last words. A moment later, you sink down onto the crummy black capes that are piled on the floor.

Since you aren't dead, your vampire body never decays. For a small fee, your parents let Mr. Reuterly display you in his store window. A sign beside you reads VAMPIRE WITH BRACES. Reuterly dresses you up in one of the capes from Vampire in a Can.

You were right. The costume *does* make you look like a nerd!

THE END

58

You desperately thirst for . . . that red cranberry juice in the fridge. But when you sip some, you have to spit it out. It tastes *lousy*.

"I feel weird," you moan. "How come the room got so bright? The light is killing my eyes."

Before Gabe can answer, you race to your room at the back of the house. You close all the blinds. When Gabe catches up with you, you slam the door and turn off the light. You both stand in darkness.

"Maybe you're coming down with the flu," Gabe suggests, popping some bubblegum into his mouth.

You hope it's only the flu. But you have a bad feeling. . . .

You slowly turn and gaze into the mirror.

"No!" you cry when you see what's staring back.

Turn to PAGE 72.

Hmmm. Why would Weniger take your dog into the movies?

The answer is easy: Weniger is nuts!

"Maybe you're right," you agree. "Maybe he went into the movies."

"Yeah," Gabe says with a sigh. "Too bad we can't follow him. I don't have any money."

Neither do you. But you know another way in.

You lead Gabe around to the back of the shopping center — to the emergency exit door. "They always keep it unlocked in case of fire," you explain.

You pull open the door, and the two of you slip into the darkened theater.

As you scan the seats, you feel two large, heavy hands on your neck. You're jerked backwards.

Someone is grabbing you from behind!

Turn to PAGE 77.

"Don't go," Gabe whispers loudly. "It's a trap!"

Carmine squints at you. "Look," he snaps. "*You* came here for help. Do you want it or not?"

"Uh, yeah," you say. But you whisper to Gabe, "If I'm not back in ten minutes, come looking for me."

"Are you nuts?" Gabe whispers back. "If you're not back in *five*, I'm calling the police!"

You nod. Then you follow Carmine through the NO ADMITTANCE door.

It leads into a long, dark, twisting hallway.

"Where are we going?" you ask anxiously.

"That's for me to know and you to find out," Carmine says with a cold laugh.

Uh-oh. I don't like this, you think.

Carmine opens a door leading into a cavernous space. The warehouse. The only light comes from some dim red bulbs.

At the far end of the room, you see a row of coffins!

Don't scream. Just hurry to PAGE 68.

Your instincts tell you to hide.

So you quickly jump into the open grave and crouch down.

CRUNCH. CRACK.

Footsteps! They come closer.

CRACCCCKKK. CRUSHMASHH.

What is that? you wonder. It sounds like someone dragging something through the woods.

You crouch lower, huddling in one corner of the grave.

All at once, something large and heavy is heaved into the grave. It lands on your head.

THUD.

It's about the size of . . .

"No!" you scream when you realize what it is.

Turn to PAGE 100.

Drink lots of liquids.

But for you, only one beverage will hit the spot: blood!

You're so desperate, you're tempted to bite your pet poodle, Fifi, on the neck. But instead, you spend the day with the blinds drawn, snoozing.

After school, Gabe comes over.

"I don't think this vampire thing is wearing off," you tell him. "We've got to go back to Mr. Reuterly's store."

"Fine." Gabe shrugs. "But stay away from the Eyeball Man. His glass eye is creepy."

Gabe heads to your bedroom door and yanks it open wide.

A beam of daylight streams into your room from the hall. You twist away, feeling a searing pain.

"No! Close the door — quick!" you shout at Gabe. "The light is killing me!"

Turn to PAGE 54.

Your mom hurries out of the room. When she returns a minute later, your dad is with her. Your dad, the dentist!

"Hey, kiddo," he says. A little dental mirror peeps above his shirt pocket. "Got a problem with a tooth?"

"No!" you shout at him. "I don't have a problem with a tooth. I've got fangs! Don't you get it? I've turned into a vampire!"

Your parents exchange a worried glance. "I know they seem like fangs to you," your dad says. "I know how kids your age feel. You're self-conscious about your looks. I'll take you to my office right now — and before you know it, we'll have the problem under control."

"Now?" you say. "But it's ten o'clock at night!"

"Get in the car," he orders.

Turn to PAGE 94.

"See? I told you I have fangs!" you exclaim to your mom.

"Sorry," she says, laughing. "I don't see any fangs. But you certainly need to brush those teeth!"

No fangs? Brush your teeth?

You rush to the mirror. You see yourself! Your reflection is back! And the fangs are gone.

"Yes!" you cry, pumping a fist in the air. "The garlic worked! I'm normal again!"

Gabe races to the mirror and checks out his own reflection.

"Yeah!" he cheers. "We're normal! We're normal!"

"Thank goodness!" you rejoice. "Because being a vampire is a real pain in the neck!"

THE END

"I'm not an animal," you tell Gabe in a low, animal-like voice. "I'm a vampire — a vampire with braces. Since I can't bite anyone, I have to get blood any way I can."

"Whatever," Gabe says. You can see he's still grossed out.

"If you don't like it, you don't have to be my friend anymore," you tell him.

Gabe shrugs. "No, I'll be your friend. I just won't invite you over for family dinners anymore."

"Yeah, I see your point," you admit, licking a last drop of steak blood from your pinkie.

"But what about when your dad takes off the braces?" Gabe asks. "What if you start biting people again?"

Turn to PAGE 101.

The old woman smiles at you. Fangs hang down over her wrinkled old lips.

You're caught. Trapped in a cell, in a basement full of vampires. And a hideous female vampire is blocking the door!

You hate having to do this to an old woman, but . . .

You drive your shoulder into her.

She doesn't budge. Not an inch. You bounce backwards. "Wow!" you exclaim. "Did you ever think of playing for the Dallas Cowboys?"

"Shhh!" she says urgently, putting a finger to her lips. "They'll hear you!"

She glances over her shoulder to be sure no one's coming. Then she takes the black iron key from the door. She uses it to unlock Gabe's chains.

"If you want my help, come with me," she whispers. She hobbles to the door and motions for you to follow.

You glance at Gabe. He shrugs. His expression is cool and distant. Like he doesn't care what happens.

You'll have to decide on your own.

If you trust the old woman, turn to PAGE 128.
If you want to lock her in the cell, turn to PAGE 11.

Open the packet? you wonder.

"No, I'll pass," you decide, shaking your head. "I mean, seriously. It might be poison or something."

Gabe tosses you the packet nervously.

"This gives me the creeps," he says. "I don't even want to hold it."

"Don't give it to me," you object, throwing it back to him.

Gabe lets it fall to the floor. "*I* don't want it."

Just then, your dog comes trotting into the room. She snatches up the packet in her teeth.

"Hey — no, Fifi!" you scold your dog, a big black poodle. "Put that down. No!"

But you're too late. Fifi tears into the packet. Something red drips from her mouth.

"Yuck!" Gabe says. "She's eating it! And it looks like blood!"

Turn to PAGE 83.

"In here," Herman Carmine says, motioning for you to come in.

"How stupid do you think I look?" you sputter. You turn and run. Back through the twisting hallway. Back to the office where you left Gabe. . . .

Except — there's no Gabe.

Where is he? Did he get scared and leave?

No. He'd never leave without you. He's a loyal friend. Usually.

Did he come looking for you?

But you weren't even gone five minutes.

Without warning, the NO ADMITTANCE door slams behind you. Then you hear a scream. You'd know that scream anywhere! It's Gabe's!

Oh, no! Gabe didn't leave. He was kidnapped!

Gabe was right. You walked into a trap. You brought these vampires some fresh blood!

What do I do now? you moan silently.

If you search the building for Gabe, turn to PAGE 104.

If you go home to get help, turn to PAGE 10.

"Don't bite him! That's my best friend!" you shout.

But it's too late. Mr. Reuterly's fangs are already piercing Gabe's neck. You hear a horrible slurping sound. Gabe struggles and kicks like a madman.

"Stop!" you scream, kicking Reuterly in the shins.

Finally he drops Gabe on the doorstep, like an empty can of soda.

Turn to PAGE 90.

"Sanguine" means "*bloody*"?

Yikes!

"You're right," you decide. "I'd better not go there."

Gabe lets out a sigh of relief. "Good. But now what?"

"I'm going home to get some sleep. Maybe this thing will wear off by the morning," you answer.

"What if it doesn't?" Gabe asks.

"Then we'll try one of your other ideas," you reply. "Call me tomorrow."

You hurry home and curl up in bed. As you pull the covers up, you snag the blanket on your fangs.

This bites, you think as you drift off to sleep.

Wake up on PAGE 126.

"What's going on?" you ask Mrs. Weniger. "Where are all the pets?"

"We had a small accident," she answers. "I'll be getting some new animals by the end of the week."

"Even the fish are gone!" you exclaim.

"I know." Mrs. Weniger nods. "And they're cold-blooded. I didn't think —"

Then she stops herself.

"Sorry," she says. "Come back next week."

She pushes you out the door.

"What did she mean about the fish being cold-blooded?" Gabe asks when you're outside.

You shudder. "I think Fifi must have bitten all her animals. The fish too. Even though their blood is cold. Usually, vampires prefer a warm meal."

"That answer sounds pretty fishy," Gabe says. "Hey — where are you going?"

"To Weniger's house," you answer as you hop on your bike.

"How come?" Gabe asks.

"Because he had Fifi yesterday," you call, riding away. "And I'll bet he still has her!"

Turn to PAGE 123.

You stare into the mirror.

Nothing stares back at you.

Of course, that's because the room is pitch-black. But when you snap on the desk lamp, your worst fear comes true.

You have no reflection. You're not there!

Gabe peers into the mirror. He stops chewing his gum.

"Whoa!" he breathes. "What happened to you?"

You know what happened. You know why you have no reflection in the mirror.

You're a vampire!

"You've got to help me, Gabe," you groan.

"Yikes!" Gabe cries. "What's happening to your teeth?"

"My teeth?" you say weakly. You touch your canines.

With a sickening shock, you feel them growing! Turning into long, pointy fangs!

"I'm so thirsty!" you moan. "For blood!" You stare longingly at Gabe's neck.

"Keep away from me!" Gabe cries, stumbling backwards.

You want to, you need to — but can you?

Can you drink your best friend's blood?

If you bite Gabe, turn to PAGE 87.
If you don't bite him, turn to PAGE 103.

You scream and scream. But no one is listening. Whoever is up there keeps shoveling in dirt. The earth drops in faster and faster. It fills your mouth until you can no longer scream.

In minutes, you're completely buried. You know you should *really* panic now. But instead, a warm, cozy feeling sweeps over you.

Oh, well, you think as you settle into the comfortable grave. This is a perfect place for a nap. After all this excitement, you're feeling tired.

Dead tired.

THE END

In the next few moments, Mr. Reuterly drains your blood and leaves you for dead in the open grave.

Sometimes it just doesn't pay to stick your neck out for your friends.

THE END

"Fifi!" you cry. "Here, girl!"

But she doesn't appear. She's long gone.

There's no point searching for Fifi. She could be anywhere! You slink back into the house and collapse on the living room sofa. When you see her water bowl, you feel a pang in your heart.

You also feel a pang in your head from when Fifi slammed you to the floor.

Every once in a while, you check the front yard to see if your dog has come home. She hasn't. You and Gabe spend the afternoon watching reruns of *Lassie* on TV.

Just after sunset, the phone rings.

A cranky-sounding caller grumbles, "Your dog is out in my front yard howling. Come and get her, quick — before I lose my temper and call the police!"

Hurry to PAGE 27.

Panting, you run the last block to Scary Stuff. You get there just as Mr. Reuterly is turning away to leave. His balding head shines in the moonlight.

"Excuse me, Mr. Eye — I mean, Mr. Reuterly," you call.

He turns around and glares at you. "Yes?" he growls.

"Uh, I bought this c-costume," you stammer, showing him the Vampire in a Can. "And, um, I accidentally opened the packet inside. And, uh, well, drank the stuff in it."

Mr. Reuterly points to the label on the side of the can. "See this?" he says. "There's a number to call if you have a problem. Now I must be going. Good night — and good luck," he adds with a mysterious smirk.

As Mr. Reuterly walks away, you and Gabe huddle under a streetlight. You read a message written on the can's label.

It says: FOR PROBLEMS WITH THIS COSTUME, CALL 555-VAMPIRE. CALLS ACCEPTED *AFTER DARK ONLY!*

Turn to PAGE 39.

"Caught you!" a voice exclaims.

You try to pull away, but he's holding you too tightly.

Weniger's going to murder me, you think.

Finally the man spins you around.

Uh-oh. It's not Mr. Weniger. It's the movie theater manager!

"I saw you sneaking in the exit," he whispers angrily. "Now I'm going to call your parents!"

"No, please," you plead. "We were just . . ."

Gabe interrupts. "Look! There he is!"

Gabe is pointing to a man sitting in the middle row. In the dark theater, you can't tell if it's Weniger.

But you *can* see the four-legged customer beside him.

It's Fifi, your dog!

Turn to PAGE 25.

"No!" you snap at your mom. You pull away, so she can't look in your mouth. You don't want her to see the fangs. "I mean, uh, it's not my throat or anything," you explain. "It's my stomach. I think I'm going to throw up."

"Oh, dear," your mom says, backing away.

Your mom is kind of squeamish about throwing up.

"In fact . . ." you groan. Leaping out of bed, you run to the bathroom and slam the door. You quietly fill a glass with water.

Then, really loudly, you make the sound of throwing up.

At the same time, you pour the whole glass of water down the toilet.

It sounds just like the real thing!

Wipe your mouth and then turn to PAGE 19.

While the vampires lick blood from Countess Yvonne, you dart away. Toward the back of the room.

Then you spot something. A big wooden door, locked with an ancient iron lock. An old key is in the door.

It looks like a prison cell. You turn the key and open the door.

Gabe is chained by his hands and feet to the back wall!

"Gabe!" you cry softly.

He stares at you coldly.

"Are you okay?" you ask him.

In answer, he shows you his neck.

"Oh, no!" you cry. There, freshly pierced, are two little holes. Two tiny marks that can mean only one thing.

He's been bitten by a vampire!

Turn to PAGE 51.

80

"I don't like that look on your face," Gabe says, backing away from you. "What are you going to do?"

You give Gabe a sly smile. "I'm just going to have a little fun — as a vampire."

"Are you nuts?" Gabe sputters. "You can't do that! You can't go around biting people and drinking their blood!"

"Don't worry," you tell Gabe. "I won't bite *you*. But how about people we hate? Like Robbie Morgan? Or Mrs. Winesap?"

Mrs. Winesap lives down the block. She kept your Frisbee once when it landed in her flower garden.

Gabe laughs a sort of sick, weak laugh. "That old bat?" he says. "She *is* pretty mean, but . . ."

"Leave it to me," you tell Gabe. "But right now, I've got to get some sleep."

You glance around your room for a comfortable place to sleep. You finally spot one and climb into position — hanging upside down from a chin-up bar in your doorway. With your arms folded across your chest like a bat!

Turn to PAGE 14.

"It's missing!" you cry in horror.

"Yeah, but look," Gabe whispers. "There's a loose torn page tucked in the back of the book."

The match you're holding is burning your fingers.

Gabe yanks out the missing page. It's the one you need! You read:

FOR FOUR HOURS AND A DAY
DRINK GARLIC AND WATER
NO MORE
AND EAT NOTHING.

Then the match goes out.

"Hmm. So this says *not* to drink garlic and water," Gabe remarks.

"No," you argue. "It says drink garlic and water, no more. That means drink nothing *but* garlic and water."

"That's nuts," Gabe retorts. "But it won't matter — unless we can get out of here."

The cell door swings open. And your heart sinks.

Turn to PAGE 4.

You tear down the dark, quiet street. You can hear your dad chasing you. But you're fast. And he's out of shape. You soon leave him far behind.

You hurry to Gabe's house and throw pebbles at his bedroom window to get his attention.

"Gabe!" you whisper loudly, throwing more pebbles.

CRASH.

Oops. That was a rock, not a pebble.

Turn to PAGE 43.

Fifi slurps up the red liquid in the packet.

"No, Fifi!" you scold, trying to take it away.

"GRRRRR!"

She growls at you angrily, her eyes gleaming.

"Uh-oh," Gabe says. "What's she doing that for?"

"I don't know," you answer, worried. Fifi has never growled at you in her life.

"GRRRRRRR!"

When the packet is empty, Fifi drops it to the floor. Then she barks and runs to the kitchen door. She jumps against the door with her front paws, clawing and digging.

"I think she wants out," Gabe whispers.

"Too bad," you say. "She can't go out if she's going to act like this."

"GRRRRR! RUFFF! RUFFF!"

Fifi snarls and barks at you, baring her teeth.

"Oh, no!" you cry. You can't believe what you're seeing. "She's growing fangs!"

Try to control your dog on PAGE 95.

All heads in the room turn toward you.

"Welcome," a woman calls out. She's wearing a long red velvet gown. "We've been expecting you."

Everyone smiles at you. Their fangs glisten.

You can't speak. Can't run. Can't do anything except take in the horrible scene.

The room is stuffed with coffins, candelabras, and vampires. Some of them are lounging in their coffins, reading magazines and newspapers. A few hang upside down from the rafters, like bats.

"How lovely of you to join us," the woman coos. "I'm Countess Yvonne. Won't you come in and have something to drink?"

She sweeps her arm toward a huge stone table. On it are silver goblets filled with a red liquid.

"No, thanks," you say. "Where's Gabe? What have you done with him?"

"We'll answer all your questions," Countess Yvonne replies. "But first — have one drink."

If you drink the red liquid, turn to PAGE 49.
If you refuse, turn to PAGE 5.

I'm such a loser vampire, you think.

You stumble from Mrs. Winesap's house and walk aimlessly. In a daze.

When you look up, you find you've entered a cemetery!

And you're standing next to an open grave.

You peer in. The grave is empty.

CRACK!

You hear a sound behind you.

Something tells you to get out of there — fast.

But the empty grave pulls you to it. Graves. They seem so cozy. So comforting. So homey.

The footsteps come closer.

Make a choice before it's too late. Quick!

If you hide in the open grave, turn to PAGE 61.
If you stay and face whoever is coming, turn to PAGE 29.

You touch the bite marks on your neck.

"Does that hurt?" Gabe asks.

You shrug. "Not much. I wonder where Fifi went? Oh, well. She'll probably come home later tonight. Before sunrise."

Gabe gives you a strange look. "I'm going back to my house now," he says nervously.

If you didn't know better, you'd swear Gabe was afraid of you. Heh, heh!

"So I'll see you on Saturday night? For Halloween?" he asks.

You grin, letting your fangs show. Then you reach for Gabe.

"Nope," you say. "For you, Halloween is starting right now!"

THE END

You gaze at Gabe's neck as if it were a tasty milk shake. "I need some liquid refreshment," you say, drooling.

"Get away from me!" he shrieks, taking off.

You run after him and corner him in the kitchen.

"I know what'll stop a vampire," he wheezes. He reaches into the freezer and pulls out . . .

A steak! Gabe rams the frozen filet mignon into your chest.

"You need a *stake* to kill a vampire," you snarl. "That's S-T-A-K-E, dope." You reach for his neck again.

Gabe yanks out his bubblegum and jams it into your mouth. Smart move! By the time you unstick the gum from your fangs, you've come to your senses.

"Sorry, Gabe," you say. "I lost my head."

He accepts your apology. But you can see he still doesn't trust you. Not completely.

You bury your face in your hands. "What am I going to do? I'm a vampire! A cruddy, bloodsucking vampire!"

Turn to PAGE 99.

"Sit down and relax!" Gabe shouts.

He pulls you back down on the couch.

"What are you doing?" he demands.

"Uh . . . I was . . . uh, trying to turn into a bat and fly out of here," you admit sheepishly.

"Oh, man." Gabe shakes his head. "We're in deep trouble."

He picks up the remote and turns off the videotape.

"Okay," he announces. "Obviously this video thing isn't working."

"You're right," you agree. "So now what?"

"Now you pick one of the other ideas I came up with," he says matter-of-factly.

He's right. You hate it when he's right.

Go back to PAGE 116 and pick again from the choices at the bottom of the page.

As you round the corner of the factory, you see a huge garage door. You both try to slide the door up. But it's locked.

"Forget it," Gabe orders. "Let's use the *front* door. Like regular human beings."

You start to follow your friend.

But all of a sudden you feel a new sensation. You're changing again — from deep *inside*.

A moment later, you have the strongest urge to fold your arms across your chest, like a bat. Something tells you that if you *do*, you'll be able to fly!

"Use the front door — like human beings?" You repeat Gabe's words. "But what if I'm *not* human?"

Gabe grabs your arm. "You're my best fiend — er, friend. I know you're human," he insists. "Come on."

If you go with Gabe, turn to PAGE 12.
If you try to become a bat, turn to PAGE 129.

90

"You killed my best friend!" you scream at Mr. Reuterly.

"He's not dead," Mr. Reuterly answers calmly. "He's just — changing. Into one of us."

"What's happening?" a voice calls from inside the house. You glance up and see Robbie at the front door.

Mr. Reuterly grabs Robbie and drains his blood. Then he drops Robbie on the doorstep beside Gabe.

"Aaah." Reuterly sighs. "Well, I'm off. I think I'll walk — I always have trouble flying after a heavy meal." He waves. "See ya, kid."

You gaze into Gabe's eyes and watch his last flicker of humanity fading. "What are you doing at Robbie's house?" you ask.

"I came to warn him," Gabe answers. "About you."

Just then a car pulls into the driveway. Oh, no. Robbie's parents are home!

If you think you can talk your way out of this, turn to PAGE 108.

If you'd rather not try, run to PAGE 23.

You ignore Gabe's warning.

"I *have* to go," you tell him as you start walking. "You don't understand. I don't *want* to be a vampire!"

"Okay," Gabe answers. "Then I'm coming with you."

An hour later you're in a deserted part of town. An old brick factory stands at 999 Sanguine Road.

The whole building is dark. On the front door is a sign reading OFFICE. RING BELL.

"Whoa!" Gabe cries. "Check out the bats!"

Overhead, dozens of tiny bats circle wildly. They fly into a high, open window at the back of the factory.

You feel drawn to them. Strange. The only other bat you've ever been attached to was your old Louisville Slugger.

"We should follow the bats," you say. "Let's check if we can get in around the back."

"No," Gabe begs. "Let's ring the front bell."

If you follow the bats, turn to PAGE 44.
If you go to the front door, turn to PAGE 12.

Oops. It's too late. You're so weak and tired, you turned the pages too slowly.

Which means that you're much too weak to pull Carrie away from your dad.

Helplessly, you watch her drain the life out of him. When she's done, she drops his body on the pavement.

"Carrie!" you cry as you slump against a car, unable to stand any longer. "What . . . ?"

"Vampire in a Can," Carrie answers, guessing your question. "I bought it from Scary Stuff. Just like you."

"But — but — do you *like* being a vampire?" you ask.

"Hel-*lo*! I'm going to stay young and pretty forever," she replies. "Can anything be more awesome?"

She opens a compact. Then she rolls her eyes. "I forgot. I can't see myself in the mirror. Do I have any blood on my face?"

You numbly point to the corner of her mouth.

"Thanks," she murmurs, and wipes away a smear of blood with a tissue. "For sure I won't be seeing you at school anymore — unless they start offering night classes!"

Turn to PAGE 98.

In a panic, you decide to try for the house.
"YIP! BARK! WOOF!"
The dogs are at your heels again as you race toward the sliding-glass doors.
Uh-oh. Locked!
Well, this looks like the wrong choice.
But if you hurry, maybe you can still make it to the garage.

Hurry to PAGE 137.

94

Dad drags you to his dental office late at night.

While you sit in the dentist's chair, he works on your fangs. First he grinds them down. Then he puts braces on your teeth. By the time he's done, your mouth is so full of metal, you can hardly talk.

"Now, those 'fangs,' as you call them, shouldn't bother you anymore," your dad declares.

"Ohshf? Rreaphly?" you say.

One thing hasn't changed, though. Your thirst.

Your whole body feels weak. Weak from the thirst that only blood will satisfy.

If I don't get blood, I'll die, you think.

You eye your dad's neck, and start to drool. The urge to bite him is so strong, you can hardly resist.

Do you dare to puncture Pop?

If you bite your dad, turn to PAGE 130.

If you wait to bite the first person you see who isn't a family member, turn to PAGE 106.

Fifi snarls at you viciously. Her lips curl back, exposing new, curved fangs. They're at least twice as long as they used to be — and razor sharp.

Like a vampire's.

Fifi lunges at you. You back up, shocked. Your own dog is attacking you!

With her weight, Fifi easily knocks you down. For an instant, you're sure she's going to bite your neck.

You roll away from her, cowering.

"HOWWWWWWL!"

Her howling moan sounds crazy. She leaps at the kitchen door one more time. This time she breaks it down!

"S-S-Stop her!" Gabe stutters.

You're so shaken, you stand there for a second.

Then you grab Fifi's leash. "Come on!" you shout, snapping out of it. "We've got to get her back."

But just as you start to leave, the phone rings.

If you answer the phone, turn to PAGE 15.
If you let it ring and run after Fifi, turn to PAGE 41.

"Hey, parrot!" you shout. "Polly want a cracker?"

"Cracker?" the parrot squawks. "I want your blood!"

"Hold on!" you cry. "How'd you get to be a vampire?"

"Oh!" The parrot lands on the back of a chair. "That's a long story," it says.

"Give me the short version," you answer. "I don't have all day."

"You've got a lot less time than you think," the parrot snaps. "Anyway. It was like this. Mrs. Weniger's son, Jeremy, came into the store last night with this dog. With fangs. The next thing you know, the dog was running around, biting all of us. Every single animal in the shop. Can you believe it?"

"Yes," you say impatiently. "Go on."

You wish you hadn't asked. Because the story gets worse.

Much worse.

Turn to PAGE 125.

"Yeoowww!" your dad screams. "Are you crazy, you little brat?"

He stands up so fast, he pulls you out of the dentist's chair. You stumble backwards. Horror washes over you.

You tried to suck your dad's blood! Gross! That never happens! Not even in the cheesiest horror movies.

You stare at his neck. Wait! It's scratched up, but he's not bleeding.

Your braces got in the way. And your fangs are no longer sharp enough to puncture his skin.

"I'm . . . I'm sorry!" you cry.

Your dad looks angry. Worse than when you put tinfoil in the microwave.

You run out of the office. This is like being in a weird GOOSEBUMPS book, you think. The kind that sends you chasing in circles. Maybe I'm just having a bad dream.

Unfortunately for you, this is real.

Turn to PAGE 82.

Carrie glides away. Weak beyond belief, you slide to the ground. Consciousness fades.

The good news is that you aren't really dead. Vampires can live forever in this weakened state.

The bad news is that you're declared legally dead, anyway. So your mom has you cremated.

After you've been burned to ashes, the undertaker saves your fangs. "These will be perfect for my son's Halloween vampire costume!" he says happily.

THE END

Gabe starts pacing around the room.

"The way I see it, you've got three choices," he begins.

"Choice number one: Go back to where you bought this stupid costume, and ask the Eyeball Man to help. It's his fault you're a vampire, right? He sold it to you."

"Maybe," you agree. "But what if he can't help? What else?"

"Choice number two: We do some research," Gabe continues. "You know — rent a bunch of vampire movies. Read up on ghouls like you — no offense — at the library. Stuff like that. Maybe we'll find out how to cure you."

"That sounds good. But it might take too long," you reply. "What's my third choice?"

"The third choice is the most dangerous," Gabe announces solemnly.

Turn to PAGE 116.

100

Someone's thrown a dead body into the grave!

Yeech! Pinned down by a creepy corpse. You should never pay attention to your instincts!

You can't budge the body. You can hardly move. "Help!" you cry. "Get me out of here! Helllppp!"

In answer, shovelfuls of wet earth rain down on your head.

You're being buried alive!

Turn to PAGE 73.

"No problemo," you tell him. "I'm never getting the braces off. Ever."

"Cool," Gabe says, nodding. "The only question I have is this. What are you going to be for Halloween?"

"Easy," you answer. "I'm going to pretend I'm human!"

THE END

102

Oh, no, you think. NO!

For an instant, you close your eyes. You don't want to look.

But even with your eyes closed, you can imagine what happened.

Fifi bit the Berklines' dog.

No. It's worse than that, you have to admit. Much worse.

Fifi bit Buttermilk — and drank his blood!

"Buttermilk, poor boy," you say, petting him.

Is he dead? you wonder. You place your ear close to his chest and listen.

All at once, the golden retriever turns his head, opens his mouth, and snaps in your face!

Turn to PAGE 3.

You don't want to leave unsightly fang marks on your best friend's neck, do you?

On the other hand, what's the point of being one of the undead if you can't drink the blood of a human now and then?

And Gabe has plenty of blood to spare. . . .

Go on. Take a little bite. Just a nibble. . . .

Go to PAGE 87 and bite Gabe, if you dare!

104

In a panic, you pick up a chair. You hurl it through the window of the NO ADMITTANCE door. Then you reach through the broken glass and unlock the door from the other side.

You've got to find Gabe. No matter how dangerous it is, you've got to find your friend — and fast!

You hurry down the long, twisting hallway. Shattered glass crunches under your feet. In the dark, you sense the right direction. Toward the door that Carmine opened. The one leading to the coffins.

Vampires *sleep* in coffins, you think, as you near the door.

You slowly turn the knob.

SQUEEK! Uh-oh! Are the door's hinges rusty? No, it's only a mouse.

The door opens noiselessly.

You lift your foot and step across the threshold. But as you put your weight down, the wooden floor gives way.

And you start to fall!

Fall all the way to PAGE 117.

The next few moments are a blur. You struggle to push your huge dog away.

Suddenly, someone pulls the dog off you.

It's Weniger!

Weniger? Saving your life?

Fifi runs howling out of the movie theater.

Your neck is throbbing. And your dog — your vampire dog — is gone.

You run down the aisle, dribbling blood. You've got to catch her!

"Wait!" Mr. Weniger calls. He and Gabe catch up to you outside the theater.

"I'm sorry," Weniger tells you. "I thought I could help. You see, I'm a dog psychologist."

"Huh?" Gabe says, laughing. "A doggie shrink?"

"Yes," Weniger goes on. "I noticed that your dog thinks she's a vampire. So I brought her to this movie to show what a horrible life she was choosing for herself. Unfortunately, she enjoyed the film. I'm afraid my plan backfired."

Turn to PAGE 47.

106

You decide not to bite your dad.

You can wait, can't you? Just a few minutes longer . . .

Although the need for blood is twisting your stomach into a tortured, painful lump.

Maybe I'll find a victim in the parking lot when we go outside, you tell yourself.

Your dad locks up the office, and you walk to his car.

Rats, you think. There isn't a soul in sight.

Until . . .

Out of the corner of your eye, you see a flicker of movement. A figure lurks behind a lamppost. A figure dressed in black.

Before you can react, the figure darts out and lunges at your dad!

Under the lamplight, you see who it is.

Carrie Mosher — a girl from your school!

"Aaaahhh!" your dad screams as Carrie sinks her long white fangs into his flesh!

Hurry to PAGE 92 — before it's too late to save your dad!

You decide you want Gabe to ring the bell.

Hold on.

What kind of a wimp-out is that?

And what are you afraid of, anyway? The *doorbell* might jump out and bite you?

Face it. You're never going to have an exciting adventure if you keep letting your best friend do everything!

You'll just go on making more wimpy decisions. And that will eventually lead you to another page like this one! A page where you're stuck facing the two worst words in the world —

THE END

You think you can *talk* your way out of this?

Hah! That's a good one!

Just picture it. Two bodies. Each with two small holes in the side of the neck.

And you've got two fangs.

It's a no-brainer.

Mr. and Mrs. Morgan call the police. You're hauled off to jail.

Your own parents are so ashamed, they won't even testify as character witnesses for you at the trial! The jury quickly convicts you of double murder.

You get a life sentence. Well, at least you'll have plenty of victims in jail, you think.

Unfortunately, they put you in solitary confinement. Permanently. You sit in your tiny cell, growing weaker and weaker. But you can never die. For you, a life sentence is *really* an eternity.

THE END

"Let's check out the pet store," you tell Gabe. You take off in that direction.

But when you reach the door, the pet store owner is locking up.

"Hey!" you call, knocking on the glass. "It says on your door that you're open until nine o'clock P.M.!"

"Not tonight," the owner mouths, waving you away.

Inside, you can hear parrots screeching wildly, dogs yipping, cats screaming. All the animals are going bonkers.

The owner waves you away again. She's a strange-looking elderly woman with green eyeglasses and messy, bleached hair.

"Doesn't she look like — like Weniger?" you ask.

Gabe peers at the woman. He gasps.

"Yeah!" he agrees. "You're right! She looks just like Weniger — in a wig and a dress!"

Turn to PAGE 55.

110

You join the other vampires and lick the blood.

Hope you enjoy the thrill. Because you just failed the taste test. The right answer is: Lick blood off someone's face? Gross me out!

Before your friends find out you picked this ending, close the book. That's right, shut it now! And don't even think of opening it again until you've said, "It is not normal to drink blood," five times.

But say it to yourself.

Because if your friends hear you chanting "It is not normal to drink blood," they'll think you're pretty weird.

They might even begin to wonder if you're a vampire!

Hey. On second thought . . . are you?

Nah. No way. You couldn't be.

Could you?

THE END

111

As the moon rises, you and Gabe approach Weniger's house. In the distance, you hear Fifi howling. Until you step up to the front door.

Then the howling stops.

There are no lights on inside. And Fifi is nowhere in sight.

"Ring the bell," Gabe orders, pointing.

You ring it three times before Weniger finally answers.

"Yeah? What is it?" he asks gruffly.

Uh-oh. He has two small marks on the side of his neck.

"Uh, Mr. W-Weniger," you stammer. "You called me about my dog, remember? The big black poodle. Where is she?"

"I didn't call you," Weniger snaps. "I don't know what you're talking about."

Then he slams the door in your face.

"Whoa," Gabe mutters. "I don't believe that guy! Ring the bell again."

"*You* ring it," you say fearfully.

If you want Gabe to ring the bell, turn to PAGE 107.

If you want to ring it yourself, turn to PAGE 53.

"Yessss," Mr. Reuterly hisses.

"Mr. Reuterly?" you gasp. "You're . . . you're a vampire?"

"I'm glad we see eye to eye on that." He snickers, putting his glass eye back in. "The salesman gave me quite a discount on those Vampire in a Can costumes," he adds with a soft chuckle. "He said it was because we're 'blood brothers.' Ha-ha-ha!"

"What a yuckmeister," you mutter sarcastically.

"Well, I suppose we should be talking in a more serious vein," Reuterly says. He cackles. "Vein. Get it? Vein?"

He swoops down on you suddenly. Wrapping you in his cape, he lifts you off the ground. Then he jumps — into the deep, wet grave!

This is no joke!

Go on to PAGE 119.

Your dad follows you. "There's a special plastic film on the mirror," he explains. "It's something your uncle Todd invented, to use for special effects in movies."

Your dad reaches up and peels off the plastic layer. Now you can see your reflection.

"So it was all fake?" you ask.

"We know how much you love vampires," your mom replies. "We wanted to make your birthday really special. Now, everyone into the dining room for cake!"

What a night! This has been the most amazing surprise birthday party ever.

You sit down at the table, starved and thirsty.

But when your mom pours you a glass of cherry punch, it looks exactly like blood.

"Uh, thanks, Mom," you say, "but I'm not thirsty."

"Oh, but I insist," your mom says. Her eyes glitter red.

She's a vampire!

Terrified, you turn to Gabe and your father.

They hiss and bare their fangs at you.

Oh, no! They're vampires too!

Well, this will be one birthday you'll never forget!

THE END

"Raw steak? Puh-lease," you tell Gabe. "I need the real deal. Or at least that special sauce from the packet."

"So now what?" Gabe demands.

"Let's go to Scary Stuff."

As you and Gabe rush toward Scary Stuff, dogs howl at you. Those mutts sense that you're a fellow creature of the night.

Suddenly a Doberman leaps at you, barking viciously!

Turn to PAGE 7.

You and Gabe argue about the cure. "Garlic and water — and no more," you insist. "And we can't eat anything, either. For four hours and a day."

Gabe is convinced that drinking the Garlic Spray will kill you. "After all, we're vampires!"

What if you're wrong? What if Gabe's right — and the Garlic Spray kills you?

You've got to decide.

If you drink the Garlic Spray, turn to PAGE 28.
If not, turn to PAGE 120.

116

"What's my third choice, Einstein?" you repeat.

"The third choice is to stay in your room and do nothing," Gabe says. "Hide out and hope that this vampire thing wears off. But that's dangerous because . . ."

"I know," you interrupt him. "Because what if it *doesn't* wear off? What if I *can't* stop myself from biting someone?"

"So what are you going to do?" Gabe asks quietly.

"There's a fourth choice," you tell him.

"Huh? What fourth choice?" he asks nervously.

"Maybe being a vampire is way cool." You grin evilly. "Maybe I should just go around biting people."

You see a flicker of fear in Gabe's eyes. And you love it!

Make a choice.

Choice #1: You go back to the Eyeball Man. Turn to PAGE 26.

Choice #2: You do research about vampires. Turn to PAGE 45.

Choice #3: You hide out in your room and hope the vampire thing wears off. Turn to PAGE 9.

Choice #4: You like being a vampire. Turn to PAGE 80.

A trapdoor! "Nooooo!" you scream.

You're falling!

You plummet through musty-smelling air for a few seconds. Then — *THUD!* You land on a soft, damp pile of earth.

It's pitch-dark. You feel around. The room is small. Its walls seem to be made of rough stone. No windows.

At last, your fingers find a wooden door. You try the knob. Yes! It turns!

When the door opens, you hear voices. Laughter.

Your legs tremble with fear, but you force yourself to move. You step through the door — and gasp.

Before you is an enormous hall.

Filled with vampires!

Turn to PAGE 84.

118

You crouch down in the garage to wait it out.

Outside, the dogs keep howling. Clawing at the door. They smell me, you realize in horror. They smell my blood!

Finally, an hour later, you hear Gabe's voice outside. You jump up and peer out the window.

To your surprise, he's carrying a bunch of dog biscuits. He walks straight toward the vampire dogs!

"Here, Buttermilk. Here, boy," he calls.

You watch, amazed, as Gabe tosses a dog biscuit to each vampire dog. One by one, they calm down. Their fangs shrink, then disappear. The howling stops.

Fifi comes trotting toward Gabe with her fangs dripping blood. But when Gabe gives her a dog biscuit, Fifi wags her tail. She gulps down the biscuit. Suddenly she becomes a normal, lovable dog again!

Sighing with relief, you cautiously open the garage door and come out. You give Fifi a big hug. Then you turn to Gabe. "Wow!" you exclaim. "How'd you do that?"

"I'll never tell," Gabe says mysteriously. "Unless you let me drink your blood!"

Turn to PAGE 6.

"Help!" you scream as you and the Eyeball Man fall into the open grave. You land with a thud.

"Hush!" Reuterly commands. "Do you want to wake the dead?" He laughs hard at his own dumb joke.

Then he becomes serious. "Not long ago I was ill, close to death. But the vampires came, offering to make me a blood brother. To give me eternal life. In return for selling Vampire in a Can."

"Let me go!" you cry, pushing away from him.

"Quiet," Mr. Reuterly says. "I'm trying to help you. I'll show you all the tricks of our trade — and I ask only one thing in return."

"What is it?" you ask fearfully. You know the answer isn't going to be pleasant.

But you might as well hear it. So go to PAGE 124.

"Fine. We'll do it your way," you snarl at Gabe. "We don't drink the garlic and water. And we eat nothing for four hours and a day."

"Good," Gabe replies.

"But I'm hungry already," you whine.

For the next few hours, you and Gabe just sit in your room, waiting. Hoping that you're doing the right thing.

And getting hungrier.

Your stomach starts to rumble. Your mouth is dry. Your throat is begging for liquid.

"I can't stand it anymore," you announce suddenly. "I need something to drink!"

You jump up and lunge for the door. But Gabe is faster. He leaps to his feet and blocks your way.

"No, you don't," he warns. "We made a deal."

"No deal!" you shout. "Get out of my way!"

You shove him. He starts grappling with you.

Before you know what you're doing — you bare your fangs and bite Gabe on the neck!

Turn to PAGE 33.

You dart out of the bushes and dash off into the night. You don't think about where you're going.

All you know is that you've got to get away. Away from the horror of seeing your best friend bitten — and turned into a vampire!

You're smart, so you manage to sneak through the bushes and back alleys — and escape Mr. Morgan. Pretty soon the police siren fades away.

You make your way to a town where no one knows you. You get a job at a diner. Working the night shift, of course.

A few years later, you meet and fall in love with a customer, who also turns out to be a vampire. You marry and have lots of little immortal vampires. And you live happily ever after . . . and after . . . and after . . . and after . . .

THE END

"Raw steak? It's worth a try," you tell Gabe.

He leads you to his kitchen. From the refrigerator he pulls a raw steak. "Shouldn't we cook it a little?" Gabe asks. "You don't want to get any germs."

You sneer. "You think germs bother the undead?"

"Well, when you put it that way . . ." he replies.

You pick up the meat in your hands and slurp at it. Blood drips down your face.

"Ummm. Yummm," you mumble. The cow's blood runs through you. Giving you strength. Making you feel *alive* again.

When the steak is sucked dry, you lick the plate clean.

Gabe watches, horrified. "You've turned into an animal!" he says. His eyes are filled with disgust.

Turn to PAGE 65.

When you get to Weniger's, all the shutters are closed up tight. Dead leaves lie in drifts around the lawn. The place looks spooky, like a vampire's fortress.

You go up to the front door and ring the bell.

No one answers. But the door isn't locked. It swings open when you touch it. Nervously, you step inside.

"Hello?" you call into the dark living room.

The only answer is the screech of a parrot. The bird swoops down from a tall bookshelf. It dive-bombs you, heading straight for your face.

When it opens its beak, you see fangs inside.

Oh, no! It's a vampire parrot!

You crouch down to protect yourself. At the same time, you wonder:

Can this vampire parrot talk?

If you fight off the bird, turn to PAGE 37.
If you try to talk to it, turn to PAGE 96.

124

Mr. Reuterly bares his fangs.

"I want just one thing from you," he breathes. "Blood."

Your eyes widen in fear.

"No, no," Mr. Reuterly says quickly. "Not *your* blood. You're one of us. But I'm running out of humans who trust me. Humans I can get close to. You, on the other hand, have many young human friends."

"My friends?" you whisper, horrified.

Mr. Reuterly nods. "Yes. Or your enemies — I don't care. Just get me into their homes — at night. . . ."

"You want me to betray my friends?" you ask, outraged.

"In return, I'll teach you everything you need to know about vampiring," Reuterly offers. "Because otherwise, you're bound to make mistakes. You're so young."

Mistakes? What mistakes?

If you want to hear more about his offer, turn to PAGE 31.

If you refuse to listen and you run away, turn to PAGE 52.

"Pretty soon," the chatty parrot continues, "we all felt ourselves changing. Growing fangs, getting thirsty for blood. You know. The whole nine yards."

"Then what?" you ask impatiently.

"Then Jeremy Weniger brought us all here," the parrot adds. "He said this would be a safe place for us, until he could figure out a better strategy."

"You have a big vocabulary," you comment.

"Thanks," the bird says modestly.

"So where's my dog now?" you ask.

"*Your* dog?" the parrot screeches. "That was *your* dog who bit me?"

"Uh, well . . ." you stammer.

But it's too late to make up a fib. The parrot has already begun his attack.

With one powerful swoop, he dives at your neck.

Turn to PAGE 13.

You sleep so soundly, almost nothing wakes you.

Not the phone ringing the next morning. Not your mom calling you over and over, saying the phone's for you.

Finally your mom marches into your room. She pulls open the blinds, letting the sun pour in.

"Phone for you," she says. "It's Gabe. He says he's found a cure — whatever that means."

A cure? Great! As you begin to smile, your mom yanks off your blankets.

"Come on, sleepyhead," she urges.

As bright sunlight hits your face, you screech in pain.

Oops!

Too bad your mom didn't know you were a vampire. A vampire who can't stand daylight. She just burned you to a crisp.

Good thing it's time for breakfast. Because you're toast!

THE END

SCORING FOR TEST

If you picked "a" for one or both questions, you have more good sense than we thought. Give yourself ten points for each "a" answer. But then ask yourself: "If I'm so sensible, why am I taking this dumb test?" Deduct ten points unless you can answer that question in twenty-five words or less.

If you picked "b" for one or both questions, you might not have much good sense — but you have a great sense of humor! Give yourself thirty points for each "b" answer.

If you picked "c" for one or both questions, you have no common sense — but you have a great sense of adventure. Give yourself fifty points for each "c" answer.

If you refused to take this test, give yourself one hundred points.

Add up your score. If you scored at least ten points, you passed the test and may continue reading this book.

If you *didn't* score at least ten points, whoa! Check yourself into the nearest hospital and have them test for a pulse, brainwave activity, and other signs of life.

If you passed the test, turn to PAGE 128 and follow the old woman. And trust her this time!

"Okay," you whisper to the old woman. "Let's go."

The old vampire hobbles out of the cell and turns right. She leads you to a different part of the basement.

"In here," she orders, pointing to another small, dark cell. "Chained to a table is an ancient book. It speaks of a cure for vampirism. My great-great-grandfather always swore it was foolproof."

"Why haven't *you* used it?" Gabe asks suspiciously.

The old woman smiles patiently. "Because then I would be human," she replies. "I would no longer have eternal life. I am old. So I would die."

Suddenly, you hear laughter. And footsteps.

"Hurry," the old woman pleads. "I have left one match on the table for you. Light it and read quickly. I marked the page with a ribbon. Good luck."

Then she closes the door behind her — leaving you in the dark!

Turn to PAGE 32.

"No," you tell Gabe, pulling away. "I'm going to follow the bats."

You close your eyes and fold your arms across your chest.

Gabe cries, "What are you doing?"

You don't answer. You just concentrate hard on the bats . . . and on the tingling inside you.

Suddenly, your whole body feels as if it's being crushed.

Crunched.

The whole world goes dark. You open your eyes, but nothing changes.

"I can't see!" you try to scream.

But all that comes out is a high-pitched screeching sound.

Then you open your wings and lift off the ground. You're flying!

You soar in a spiral. Up — up — up!

Soar to PAGE 134.

130

You decide to go for it and bite your dad. Hey, he's your own father. He'll understand, right?

He's tall. So you can't reach his neck, unless he bends down.

"Dad," you say, in your nicest voice "can I tell you a secret?"

"Sure," he agrees.

"I have to whisper it," you tell him. "Bend down."

Your dad shrugs and puts his head next to yours.

"Okay. What is it?" he asks patiently.

"This!" you cry.

You sink your metal-covered teeth into his neck and begin the suction action.

Turn to PAGE 97.

"Surprise!" a bunch of voices all say at once.

The living room is filled with your friends.

And Gabe is standing right in the middle!

"Happy Birthday!" everyone shouts.

"But — but — it's not my birthday until next week," you sputter, feeling totally confused.

"I know," your mom says, appearing in the kitchen doorway. "But Dad and I thought it would be more fun to give you a surprise party. *Before* Halloween."

"But what about the vampires?" you whisper to Gabe. "What about my fangs, and the warehouse, and everything?"

Gabe laughs. "That stuff you drank from the packet?" he says. "That was Mr. Reuterly's idea. It's just sugar syrup, cherry juice, and a lot of salt. He said it would make you thirsty. And then the sugar syrup coats your teeth, and makes them look longer. But the rest — that was all in your head. You just *imagined* that you wanted to drink blood!"

"But what about the mirror?" you cry. You race to the hall mirror and look in.

Your reflection is still missing!

Turn to PAGE 113.

TEST FOR GOOD SENSE

1. You've withdrawn $1,000 from the bank. You don't have any pockets, so you want someone to hold it for you. Whom should you trust? Pick one.

   a) your grandmother

   b) a kangaroo

   c) a guy with a shaved head and a tattoo that reads EX-CONS R BETTER!

2. You forget your lunch for school, and a bunch of people offer you food. Whom should you trust? Pick one.

   a) your best friend, who gives you half his sandwich

   b) a kangaroo

   c) a kid two years older than you, who says, "Take my lemonade," then turns his back, makes a horrible hacking sound, and hands you a weird-looking drink with gunk floating in it

For the answers and your score, turn to PAGE 127.

"Wow! That's probably when Reuterly became a vampire himself!" Gabe declares.

You decide to tell your mom the truth — about the Vampire in a Can, and Mr. Reuterly, and the warehouse full of vampires, and everything.

"Yeah, and I'm the Easter Bunny," your mom says when you finish. She rolls her eyes. "Halloween is coming up — not April Fools' Day!"

You plead with her: "You've got to believe me, Mom. Really! Check out my fangs."

You open your mouth wide. Your mom peers in. She gasps.

Turn to PAGE 64.

134

As you circle around, high above Gabe's head, reality hits you.

You turned yourself into a bat!

I'm blind as a bat, too, you think as you soar toward the factory window. That's where the other bats went in.

You can't see the window very well. You're not completely blind, but your eyesight is poor.

Your radar, though, tells you where the opening is.

Inside, you follow your sense of smell. It leads you to a room full of screeching bats.

They all flap their wings and circle each other. Then, one by one, they transform themselves into human form. Into vampires.

All except you.

Cold fear seeps into your little bat body as you realize:

You don't know how to change back!

Turn back to PAGE 8.

"WOOF!"

It's the familiar bark of your beloved poodle. "Fifi!" you call.

"WOOF!" Fifi races down the hall and starts licking your face.

"Help me, Fifi!" you cry.

As if she understands, Fifi starts barking at all the vampire pets. She snarls at them, growls and snaps. Even though she's a vampire, she's protecting you!

"Good dog," you coo.

But it's no use. The other animals aren't afraid of her any longer. Not since they became vampires.

In the next few moments, the bloodthirsty animals drain every drop of blood from your body.

"Oh, Fifi," you moan. "How did this happen? What went wrong?"

"Don't ask her," the parrot screeches at you. "Ask me. I'm the one who can talk."

You stare at the parrot, too surprised to speak. You're also too lifeless to listen. Which is why you'll never find out the whole story in

THE END.

You make a break for the garage.

"YIP! YIP!"

The dogs give chase. You yank open the side door and slip inside. You pull it shut. Just in time!

The frustrated dogs yap from the other side of the door. Then you see something yellow and hairy thudding against the garage door window. Buttermilk!

What if he breaks the glass? What if he gets in? Then you're dead meat.

"WOOF! WOOF! WOOF!"

You peek out the garage door window. Two more vampire dogs have joined the group. One is a Doberman. The other is a pit bull!

Where's Gabe? you wonder. Then you remember. He's waiting at your house for a phone call.

A phone call! That gives you an idea.

You rush over to the car parked in the garage and peek in the window.

Turn to PAGE 46.

Ooops! You didn't hurry fast enough.
"YIP! YIP! WOOF!"
As they bite into your neck, you think sadly, My life has really gone to the dogs.

THE END

About R.L. Stine

R.L. STINE is the most popular author in America. He is the creator of the *Goosebumps*, *Give Yourself Goosebumps*, *Fear Street*, and *Ghosts of Fear Street* series, among other popular books. He has written more than 100 scary novels for kids.

Bob lives in New York City with his wife, Jane, teenage son, Matt, and dog, Nadine.

GET
Goosebumps®
by R.L. Stine

☐ BAB45365-3	#1	Welcome to Dead House	$3.99
☐ BAB45369-6	#5	The Curse of the Mummy's Tomb	$3.99
☐ BAB49445-7	#10	The Ghost Next Door	$3.99
☐ BAB49450-3	#15	You Can't Scare Me!	$3.99
☐ BAB47742-0	#20	The Scarecrow Walks at Midnight	$3.99
☐ BAB48355-2	#25	Attack of the Mutant	$3.99
☐ BAB48348-X	#30	It Came from Beneath the Sink	$3.99
☐ BAB48349-8	#31	The Night of the Living Dummy II	$3.99
☐ BAB48344-7	#32	The Barking Ghost	$3.99
☐ BAB48345-5	#33	The Horror at Camp Jellyjam	$3.99
☐ BAB48346-3	#34	Revenge of the Lawn Gnomes	$3.99
☐ BAB48340-4	#35	A Shocker on Shock Street	$3.99
☐ BAB56873-6	#36	The Haunted Mask II	$3.99
☐ BAB56874-4	#37	The Headless Ghost	$3.99
☐ BAB56875-2	#38	The Abominable Snowman of Pasadena	$3.99
☐ BAB56876-0	#39	How I Got My Shrunken Head	$3.99
☐ BAB56877-9	#40	Night of the Living Dummy III	$3.99
☐ BAB56878-7	#41	Bad Hare Day	$3.99
☐ BAB56879-5	#42	Egg Monsters from Mars	$3.99
☐ BAB56880-9	#43	The Beast from the East	$3.99
☐ BAB56881-7	#44	Say Cheese and Die–Again!	$3.99
☐ BAB56882-5	#45	Ghost Camp	$3.99
☐ BAB56883-3	#46	How to Kill a Monster	$3.99
☐ BAB56884-1	#47	Legend of the Lost Legend	$3.99
☐ BAB56885-X	#48	Attack of the Jack-O'-Lanterns	$3.99
☐ BAB56886-8	#49	Vampire Breath	$3.99
☐ BAB56887-6	#50	Calling All Creeps	$3.99
☐ BAB56888-4	#51	Beware, the Snowman	$3.99

Scare me, thrill me, mail me GOOSEBUMPS now!

Available wherever you buy books, or use this order form. Scholastic Inc., P.O. Box 7502,
2931 East McCarty Street, Jefferson City, MO 65102

Please send me the books I have checked above. I am enclosing $_____ (please add $2.00 to cover shipping and handling). Send check or money order — no cash or C.O.D.s please.

Name _____ Age _____

Address _____

City _____ State/Zip_____

Please allow four to six weeks for delivery. Offer good in the U.S. only. Sorry,
mail orders are not available to residents of Canada. Prices subject to change.